D0578188

$\mathcal{D}$isney's
The Haunted House Party

GROLIER BOOK CLUB EDITION

First American Edition. Copyright © 1981 by Walt Disney
Productions. All rights reserved under International and
Pan-American Copyright Conventions. Published in the United
States by Random House, Inc., New York, and simultaneously
in Canada by Random House of Canada Limited, Toronto.
Originally published in Denmark as KARNEVAL I SPOGELSESHUSET
by Gutenberghus Gruppen, Copenhagen. ISBN: 0-394-85110-2
Manufactured in the United States of America
3 4 5 6   D E F G H I J K

Donald Duck was eating breakfast with
his three nephews, Huey, Dewey, and Louie.
"Here is the morning paper,
Uncle Donald," said Dewey.
"Thanks," said Donald.
"I wonder what
the news is."

Donald read the front page.

"Listen to this, boys!" he said. "There is going to be a costume party over at the haunted house. I think I will dress up like one of the Three Musketeers."

"Sounds great," said Dewey.
"Are you going to ask Daisy
to go with you?"

MORNING SUN

"Of course," said Donald. "Daisy loves
to go out with me."

He ran for the phone.

Donald called Daisy's number.
"Hi, Daisy," he said. "How about going to
the costume party? It will be a lot of fun...."

"WHAT?...
Oh. I see....
Sure. Bye."

Donald slammed down the phone.

"Who does she think she is!" he yelled.
"She says she is going to the party with
somebody else. Somebody big and strong.
Somebody who can fight off ghosts—if
the place is REALLY haunted."

"Don't worry, Uncle Donald,"
said the boys.

"Things will work out.
Don't get so upset."

"Upset?" yelled Donald. "I'm not upset!"

"Come on, fellas," said Dewey. "Let's think of a way to help Uncle Donald." Soon the boys had a perfect plan.

"We will dress up like giant bats," said Huey.

"And when the party is going strong . . ." said Dewey.

"We will fly in and scare everybody silly!" said Louie.

"And then you can chase us away!"
said Huey, Dewey, and Louie.

"Great idea, boys!" said Donald. "I will
get rid of the giant bats and be the hero
of the evening. Daisy will be sorry that
she didn't come with me!"

The night of the party came
and Donald got dressed.

He put on
his jacket . . .

. . . and his hat.

Then he tried out
his sword.

"Take that!"

Donald took a long look at himself
in the mirror.

"I will be the best-looking duck
at the party," he said.

"Bye, boys!"
called Donald.
"See you later!"

The haunted house was on the edge
of town.

Donald gulped when he saw the place.

"Maybe Daisy is right," he said.
"Maybe ghosts do live in that house!"

Donald took a deep breath and walked up
to the haunted house.

The door opened before he could knock.

Donald expected to see a ghost.

But it was only a dog dressed like a hobo.

"Hello, Donald," said the dog. "Come in."

Donald walked in and looked around.
He saw Daisy dancing with a pirate.
"Humpf!" said Donald. "She came with
Gladstone Gander! He is no stronger
than I am!"

"This is such a nice party," said Daisy
to Gladstone. "The haunted house isn't
scary at all."

But someone was watching Daisy
from the window.

It was a giant bat!

"Oh, boy," the bat said to himself.
"Daisy is in for a big surprise!"

Just then Gladstone Gander looked up.
He saw three bats at the window.
"Help! Giant bats!" he cried. "Run!"
The party guests screamed and ran.

"Wait!" called Donald.

Donald ran over to the bats
and waved his sword.

"Look at him!" said the witch.
"Donald is so brave!"

"Oh, dear," said Daisy. "I hope
he doesn't get hurt."

"Scram!" yelled Donald. "Get out of here,
you giant bats!"

Without a sound, the bats turned and
ran off into the dark night.

Donald jumped down
from the window.

He put away his sword
and dusted himself off.

"Donald is wonderful," said everyone.
"He is a hero!"

Gladstone snorted.
"Donald is just a show-off!" he said.
"Come on, Daisy. The music is starting.
Dance with a real hero. ME!"

But before long, something else happened.
All the lights went out!
"Look up there!" somebody screamed.
"At the top of the stairs!"

There stood a tall, white ghost.
Slowly it came down the stairs.
"Yeeow!" cried Gladstone. "Quick!
Everybody hide!"

Everyone dived for the nearest hiding place.
"Gladstone!" called Daisy. "Where are you?"

The ghost floated
across the room.

The ghost headed right for Daisy.
"HELP!" she cried.
No one moved . . .

. . . except Donald!

"Get away from Daisy, whoever you are!" said Donald.

He pulled out his sword.

Donald swung at the ghost.
He caught its sheet with the tip of
his sword . . .

. . . and pulled the sheet off!

"Hi, Uncle Donald," said Huey, Dewey, and Louie.

"Look!" said the clown. "It's
Donald's nephews! In bat costumes!"

"What are you doing here?" yelled Donald.
"I thought you went home after I chased
you away."

"Sorry, Uncle Donald," said Huey.
"We were just having a little fun."

"Donald knew all the time that the bats
were his nephews!" cried Gladstone Gander.
"Some hero!"
Gladstone laughed and laughed.

"Oh, brother," said Donald.

"Maybe Donald knew about the bats," said Daisy. "But he didn't know about the ghost. I didn't see YOU coming to my rescue, Gladstone."

Daisy went over to Donald and gave him a hug.

"My hero!" she said.

Gladstone felt very small
and very silly.

Without saying a word,
he left the party.

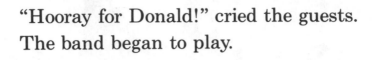

"Hooray for Donald!" cried the guests.
The band began to play.

"Come on, Daisy," said Donald. "The music
is starting. Dance with a REAL hero. ME!"